TROUBLE FOR COREY

"Ponies are so dumb!" Alice said. "And so is riding them!"

"Ponies are not dumb!" Corey shot back. "You're the one who's—"

Doc Tock gave Corey a warning look. "That's enough, Corey," she said quietly.

Corey stared down at her plate, angry tears forming in her eyes. Why had her mother told her to be quiet when it was Alice who had started the whole thing?

Corey had gotten to know Alice better, all right. And now she knew Alice well enough to see that she was the stupidest—and nastiest—girl in the world!

Corey's Secret Friend

B O N N I E B R Y A N T

Illustrated by Marcy Ramsey

A SKYLARK BOOK
NEW YORK • TORONTO • LONDON • SYDNEY • AUCKLAND

RL 3, 007–010
COREY'S SECRET FRIEND
A Bantam Skylark Book / June 1997

Skylark Books is a registered trademark of Bantam Books,
a division of Bantam Doubleday Dell Publishing Group, Inc.
Registered in U.S. Patent and Trademark Office and elsewhere.
Pony Tails is a registered trademark of Bonnie Bryant Hiller.
"USPC" and "Pony Club" are registered trademarks of The
United States Pony Clubs, Inc., at The Kentucky Horse Park,
4071 Iron Works Pike, Lexington, KY 40511-8462.

ISBN 0-553-48482-6

Published simultaneously in the United States and Canada.

Bantam Books are published by Bantam Books, a division of
Bantam Doubleday Dell Publishing Group, Inc. Its trademark,
consisting of the words "Bantam Books" and the portrayal of a
rooster, is Registered in U.S. Patent and Trademark Office and in
other countries. Marca Registrada. Bantam Books, 1540
Broadway, New York, New York 10036.

PRINTED IN THE UNITED STATES OF AMERICA

OPM   0   9   8   7   6   5   4   3   2   1

*I would like to give my special thanks
to Susan Korman for her help
in the writing of this book.*

Hi, we're the **PONY TAILS**—May Grover, Corey Takamura, and Jasmine James. We're neighbors, we're best friends, and most of all, we're pony-crazy.

My name is **May.** My pony is named Macaroni after my favorite food, macaroni and cheese. He's the sweetest pony in the world! Jasmine and Corey say he's the exact opposite of me. Of course, they're just teasing. I have two older sisters who say I'm a one-girl disaster area, but they're not teasing. Would you like some used sisters? I have two for sale.

I'm called **Corey**—short for Corinne. I live between Jasmine and May—in a lot of ways. My house is between theirs. I'm between them in personality, too. Jasmine's organized, May's forgetful, and I can be both. May's impulsive, Jasmine's cautious, and I'm just reasonable. My pony is named Samurai. He's got a white blaze on his face shaped like a samurai sword. Sam is temperamental, but he's mine and I love him.

I'm **Jasmine.** My pony is named Outlaw. His face is white, like an outlaw's mask. He can be as unpredictable as an outlaw, too, but I'd never let him go to jail because I love him to pieces! I like to ride him, and I also like to look after him. I have a baby sister named Sophie. When she gets older I'm going to teach her to ride.

So why don't you tack up and have fun with us on our pony adventures! *May Corey Jasmine*

MAY'S HOUSE   COREY'S HOUSE   JASMINE'S HOUSE

Corey's Secret Friend

1 Training Ponies

"Good job, Sam!" Corey Takamura said happily. Her pony, Samurai, had just stepped between two rocks placed in the middle of the training ring. "You did it!"

Corey was thrilled. Samurai was becoming a better-trained pony every day, but he still had a habit of misbehaving. Today he hadn't misbehaved. He had followed her instructions perfectly!

Corey patted her pony's neck to tell him how pleased she was. Then she turned to face her two best friends. They were mounted on their ponies at the opposite end of the ring. "Did you guys see that?" she called.

"We sure did," May Grover answered.

"Way to go, Sam!" Jasmine James cheered.

Corey could tell that her best friends were just as proud of Sam as she was. The three girls loved ponies and riding so much, they called themselves the Pony Tails. They were all next-door neighbors, and each of them owned her own pony. They rode together almost every day. Today they were riding in the training ring behind May's house. They were working on gaining better control of their ponies for trail riding.

Corey and Sam trotted back to the opposite end of the ring.

"Sam's doing great, Corey," May said. "I'm sure he'll be much better on next week's trail ride."

"I hope so," Corey replied. "He certainly wasn't very cooperative on Horse Wise's last trail ride."

Neither of Corey's best friends could argue with that.

Horse Wise was the name of the Pony Club at Pine Hollow Stables, where the girls took riding lessons. A few weeks earlier, all the members of Horse Wise had gone out on the trail. Most of the horses and ponies had been obedient, but Samurai had acted up the whole time. Twice he'd jumped over branches lying across the path instead of going around them. Then he'd refused to follow the other horses and ponies across a stream. Corey wanted Samurai to be prepared for the next Pony Club trail ride.

"Your turn, Jasmine," Corey said.

Jasmine nodded, then gave her Welsh pony, Outlaw, the signal to walk.

Corey watched as Jasmine used her legs and reins to steer Outlaw toward the two rocks. The Pony Tails had placed the rocks about twelve inches apart, just the way May's father had said to do it. Mr. Grover's job was to train horses, and he knew a lot about ponies, too. When Corey had told him about Sam's behavior on the trail, he had recommended this exercise. He'd said it would

3

help Sam learn how to follow very specific instructions. That was important on the trail, where riders faced lots of unexpected obstacles such as rocks, brush, and even other animals.

Outlaw approached the two rocks at a walk. But instead of following Jasmine's instruction to step between the rocks, he suddenly broke into a trot.

"No, Outlaw!" Jasmine said. She pulled firmly on the reins as he veered off to the left. "That's not what I asked you to do." She turned Outlaw around. "Come on, boy," she added in a patient voice. "We're going to try it again."

This time Outlaw did just what Jasmine asked him to do. She was smiling when she turned her pony around.

Next it was May's turn. She headed forward on her shaggy yellow pony. She had named him Macaroni because his golden coat was almost exactly the color of macaroni and cheese. Macaroni had a calm disposition and almost never misbehaved. Corey and Jasmine thought Macaroni was the complete opposite of their friend May. She was

4

unpredictable and liked to act up sometimes.

Macaroni followed May's instructions perfectly.

"Good boy, Macaroni," Corey called out as he and May trotted back to the other end. Corey wasn't surprised that Macaroni had done well, but he still deserved lots of praise. It wasn't easy for a pony to follow such specific directions.

Corey nudged Sam toward the rocks. It was their turn again.

The girls and their ponies practiced the exercise for another half hour. Then Jasmine pointed to her watch. "It's almost dinnertime," she called out.

"Already?" May groaned.

Corey groaned, too. She never wanted to stop riding, but today she especially hated to dismount. She and her mother were going out for a "special dinner," and Corey would much rather stay in the ring.

Corey slowly followed May and Jasmine as they led their ponies over to the fence. On sunny days like today, the Pony Tails liked to groom their ponies outside. That way they could talk and stay together a little while longer.

Corey tied Samurai to the fence alongside Macaroni and Outlaw. She hadn't told her friends about tonight's dinner yet. As she began checking Sam's hooves for stones, she tried to think of a way to bring up the topic.

Just then May spoke up.

"Guess what, Corey," May began. "My sister Dottie saw your mother and Mr. Lee at the movies the other night."

Corey was so startled, the hoof pick fell from her fingers. Her face burned as she bent down to pick it up.

"Dottie was with her current boy-friend, Peter," May went on. She gig-gled. "And get this, Corey. Dottie thought your mother was on a date, too!"

Jasmine carefully placed Outlaw's hoof back on the ground. "Your sister is so boy-crazy, May," she said, rolling her eyes. "She always thinks people are in love with each other!"

"I know," May agreed. "Isn't that the craziest thing you ever heard, Corey?"

May glanced at Corey, expecting to see her friend laughing at Dottie's silly remark. But Corey was concentrating so hard on picking Sam's hooves, she wasn't even looking at May.

"Corey?" Jasmine said softly.

Corey looked up. "My mom *was* on a date with Mr. Lee," she told her friends. "She's been dating Mr. Lee, I mean Kyle, a lot lately."

"What?" May screeched so loudly, all three ponies jumped.

"May!" Jasmine gave her a warning look.

May clapped a hand over her mouth. "I'm sorry, Corey," she said from behind her fingers. May hadn't meant to react like that, but she couldn't help it. She had never pictured Corey's mother, a veterinarian whom everyone called Doc Tock, going out on a date. She had especially never pictured her dating Mr. Lee, who lived across the street from the Pony Tails.

Corey sighed. "That's okay, May," she said. "I was surprised, too, when my mom first started going out with him."

"Don't you like Mr. Lee, Corey?" Jasmine asked.

Corey shrugged. "He's okay," she said. "But . . ." Then Corey told her friends what was bothering her. "My mom is making me go to Sir Loyne's Steak House tonight with her and Kyle." She made a face. "Guess who's coming with us."

"Alice?" May asked. "Poor you!" she said as Corey nodded.

Jasmine patted Corey's arm. Mr. Lee was divorced, just like Corey's mother, and his daughter, Alice, stayed with him several days each week. Alice went to Fenton Hall, a private school, so the Pony Tails didn't know her very well. But what they did know of her, they didn't like very much.

"Alice is so unfriendly," Jasmine said. "She was on my soccer team last year, and she barely said a word to anyone."

"She never waves back to me when I wave to her," May chimed in.

"Every time I see her, her nose is poked in a book," Corey said. "I mean, I like to read, too, but Alice doesn't seem

9

interested in doing anything *but* reading."

"Why is your mother making you go out to dinner with Alice and Mr. Lee?" asked May.

"She says it will help Alice and me get to know each other better," Corey explained. She sighed as she dropped her hoof pick into her grooming bucket and reached for a currycomb. "I don't want to get to know Alice better," Corey told her friends. "I don't see why my mother—"

Suddenly a terrible thought popped into her mind. She looked at her friends in a panic.

"What if my mother wants to marry Mr. Lee?" she said. "Then Alice would be my . . . stepsister!"

Jasmine tried to calm her friend down. "Your mom's only dating Mr. Lee, Corey," she pointed out. "That doesn't mean she's going to marry him."

"Right," May said. "Dating is no big deal. My sisters go out on dates all the time."

10

Corey felt a little better—until her mother came to the back door of the Takamuras' house.

"Coreeey! It's time to get ready for dinner, honey!" Doc Tock called.

"I'm coming, Mom!" Corey called back.

"Good luck, Corey," Jasmine said as Corey collected her grooming tools and untied Samurai.

"I bet it won't be so bad," May said encouragingly.

"Thanks, guys." Corey waved good-bye, then led Samurai across the Grovers' backyard, toward her own stable.

May and Jasmine said good-bye and went back to grooming their ponies.

"Poor Corey," Jasmine said. "It must feel really strange to have your mom start dating all of a sudden."

"It would feel even stranger to have Alice Lee become your stepsister all of a sudden!" May said.

Jasmine couldn't even imagine having someone as unfriendly as Alice become her stepsister. But she tried to look on the bright side. "At least Alice wouldn't cry all the time like my baby sister does," she said.

May nodded. "Alice definitely wouldn't talk on the phone all the time, the way my sisters do," she said.

Jasmine could tell that May was trying to look on the bright side, too. But as the two girls went back to grooming their ponies, they both felt doubtful about the situation. Corey's "special dinner" with Alice Lee was bound to be a disaster.

2 Dinner at Sir Loyne's

"Alice, honey," Kyle Lee suggested cheerfully, "why don't you tell Doc Tock and Corey about some of the great books you've been reading lately?"

Alice blinked at her father from behind her long, dark bangs but didn't say a word. Instead she leaned down and took a long drink of her soda through the straw.

What is her problem? Corey thought. Ever since the four of them had arrived at Sir Loyne's Steak House, Alice had barely said two words. Didn't Alice know it was rude to ignore her father like that?

"Your dad told me *Harriet the Spy* is one of your favorite books," Doc Tock said. She smiled at Alice. "Believe it or not, I read that book when I was a girl. I loved it, too."

"That's nice," Alice mumbled.

"Isn't that the book about a girl who keeps notebooks and spies on people?" Corey asked Alice. Alice stared at Corey for a second, then looked away.

Fine, Corey thought. She reached for a roll. If Alice isn't going to talk to me, I'm not going to try to talk to her anymore. This was about the fifth time this evening that Alice had completely ignored her.

"That's right, Corey," Doc Tock said, answering Corey's question. "*Harriet the Spy* is a great book. *Tuck Everlasting* is another one of my favorites. Have you read that one?" she asked Alice.

Alice nodded, then took another sip of soda.

"How about you, Corey?" Kyle asked. "Your mother tells me you like to read horse magazines. It sounds as if you like animals as much as she does."

14

"I do," Corey told him. "I might want to be a vet, too, when I grow up."

"Oh, really?" Kyle said. "It's certainly an interesting job."

"That's for sure," Corey agreed. "This week we're taking care of a sick parrot, plus there's a litter of yellow Lab puppies staying in our barn. They are *so* adora—"

"I can't stand puppies," Alice declared abruptly. Corey stopped talking in midsentence. "Especially Labrador retrievers," Alice went on, brushing her bangs off her face. "My friend Maura's puppy always jumps up on me and licks my whole face. It's totally disgusting."

Corey stared at Alice in surprise. Corey was used to being around people who loved animals the way she and her mother did. She couldn't believe that Alice didn't like Labrador retrievers or cute little puppies. Corey's own dog was a Labrador—a black one named Dracula—and Corey thought he was the best dog in the whole world.

"My Lab is really sweet," Corey told Alice. "I love it when he kisses my face."

"You love it?" Alice stared at Corey as if Corey had just said she loved to eat worms.

Corey's face flushed. This dinner was going even worse than she had expected!

Luckily, the waiter arrived before Corey had to reply. "Four Sir Loyne cheeseburgers coming up," he announced.

Normally Corey loved the burgers at Sir Loyne's. But as the waiter placed the pewter plate filled with french fries and a big cheeseburger in front of her, Corey realized she didn't want the cheeseburger. She didn't even want the french fries. All she wanted was to get away from Alice Lee.

"This looks absolutely delicious," Doc Tock said brightly.

"It certainly does," Kyle agreed. "Doesn't it, Alice?"

But Alice didn't reply. Both she and Corey silently stared at their food as Doc Tock and Kyle went on about how delicious it looked.

Corey didn't say another word until

halfway through the meal, when Doc Tock turned to her again. "What were you and your friends doing with those rocks in the Grovers' training ring this afternoon?" she asked.

Corey put down her fork. She didn't really feel like talking, but she didn't want to be rude, either.

"We were training our ponies to be good trail riders," she explained.

"How do you do that?" asked Kyle.

Corey told Kyle and her mother about the exercise May's father had suggested. For a moment she almost forgot that Alice was sitting across the table. Corey was too busy talking about her favorite subject—ponies—to think about Alice.

"Why do you want the ponies to walk between two rocks?" Kyle asked.

"Mr. Grover said it helps prepare them for the trail," Corey explained. "My Pony Club has another trail ride coming up next weekend, and I want Sam to get more used to following specific directions. You should have seen him today, Mom!" Corey went on proudly. "He did just what I asked him to do—every single time!"

"That's great, honey," said Doc Tock.

"It sounds as if Sam's come a long way," Kyle added.

"He has," Corey said. "I think all my work with him has helped—and so has Horse Wise."

"Horse Wise?" For the first time in fifteen minutes, Alice spoke. "Is that the name of a book or something?" she asked.

"It's not the name of a book!" Corey laughed out loud at Alice's remark. "Horse Wise is . . ." She was about to tell Alice it was the name of her Pony Club. But Corey's voice trailed off as she noticed the spark of anger in Alice's eyes.

"Ponies are so dumb!" Alice said. "And so is riding them! The only time I tried to go riding," she went on, "the stupid pony stepped on my foot before I even climbed into the saddle!"

Corey felt anger boil up inside her, too. "Ponies are not dumb!" she shot back. "You're the one who's—"

Doc Tock gave Corey a warning look. "That's enough, Corey," she said quietly.

Corey stared down at her plate, angry tears forming in her eyes. Why had her mother told her to be quiet when it was Alice who had started the whole thing?

A second later, Alice's fork fell to her plate with a clatter. She pushed her chair away from the table.

Kyle looked up. "Where are you going, Alice?"

"The rest room," Alice replied.

As she stomped off, Doc Tock and Kyle started talking politely about the beautiful spring weather. Corey stabbed a french fry with her fork. If Alice thinks riding ponies is dumb, then I think she's dumb! she thought angrily.

Corey didn't look up when Alice returned to the table, and neither of them said another word for the rest of the meal.

Corey had gotten to know Alice better, all right. And now she knew Alice well enough to see that she was the stupidest—and nastiest—girl in the world!

* * *

A short while later, Doc Tock opened the back door of the Lees' black Jeep.

"Thank you for dinner, Kyle," she said warmly. "Our next meal is my treat."

Our next meal? Corey thought. No way. She was never going to have dinner with Alice—or her father—again.

From the look of things, Alice wasn't eager to go out with the Takamuras again, either. She was slumped in the front seat beside her father. Her arms were folded across her chest, and an angry scowl darkened her face.

"Thank you, Kyle," Corey said, trying to be polite. She completely ignored Alice as she got out of the Jeep after Doc Tock.

"You're welcome, Corey," Kyle replied. "See you soon."

Corey was about to close the car door

when she noticed that Alice had turned around. In a low voice, Alice said something to Corey.

"Excuse me?" Corey said coldly. She hadn't heard what Alice had said, but she expected another insult.

Alice mumbled something again. This time Corey could hear the words more clearly.

"I'm sorry."

What? Corey had heard the words, but she couldn't believe her ears. Had Alice really apologized?

As Corey stood there, staring at Alice in shock, she saw Kyle reach over and pat his daughter's arm.

So that's why Alice apologized, Corey realized a second later. Her father made her do it.

Without saying anything, Corey swung the Lees' car door closed. Obviously, Alice hadn't meant the apology.

So why should I bother to accept it? thought Corey.

3 Corey's Nightmare

"Good night, Corey." A little while later, Doc Tock poked her head into Corey's room.

Corey lay on her bed reading a horse magazine. " 'Night, Mom," she mumbled without looking up.

Doc Tock came into the room and sat down on Corey's bed. "That article looks interesting." She pointed to the cover of the magazine, which showed a picture of a herd of wild ponies.

"I guess so." Corey knew she wasn't being very polite, but she didn't want to be polite. She was still angry at her mother for making her go out to dinner with Alice in the first place.

"It must be kind of strange to have your mother going out on dates all of a sudden," Doc Tock said softly. "I've been wondering if that's part of the reason why tonight's dinner didn't go very well."

Corey felt another flare of anger. "It has nothing to do with your dating, Mom. It has to do with the fact that Alice isn't very nice. I tried my best to be friends with her. She's the one who said ponies are dumb!"

"I'm sure Alice's remarks hurt your feelings, Corey," Doc Tock replied. "Maybe she—"

"Alice didn't hurt my feelings," Corey interrupted. "She just proved that she's a nasty person."

"Alice isn't a bad person just because she doesn't share your interests, Corey," Doc Tock said. "She isn't around animals all the time the way we are. Maybe she's not used to them."

Corey just glared at her mother. Doc

24

Tock had heard what Alice had said. So why was she taking Alice's side?

Finally Doc Tock stood up. "Well, thanks for coming to dinner, honey." She leaned over to give Corey a kiss. "Sleep tight."

"Good night," Corey replied.

Alice wasn't only rude to me, Corey thought as her mother left the room. She was rude to Mom, too. She was even rude to her own father! Corey had never met such an unfriendly girl.

A few minutes later, Corey tossed the magazine on the floor and turned out the light. As she settled between the sheets, she could hear the litter of puppies yipping out in the barn. The sound made her picture the round table at Sir Loyne's all over again. She could still see Alice's disgusted expression. How could someone hate being licked on the face by an adorable puppy? The dinner kept replaying in Corey's mind.

She sat up to rearrange her pillow. As she lay back down, she forced herself to think about something besides the terrible meal. She remembered that she was going to her father's apartment tomorrow to stay for the next few days. She pictured her father, with his dark hair and friendly brown eyes. Then she imagined her cheerful room at his apartment. It was decorated with pony wallpaper and lots of horse posters.

Finally Corey's eyes closed. As she drifted off to sleep, she was still picturing her room at her father's apartment. But now she was picturing herself packing up her things to come back to her mother's house . . .

"Bye, Dad," Corey said as she opened the car door. "Thanks for everything."

"See you in a few days, honey," Mr. Takamura replied.

Corey hurried up the path.

Her mother stood waiting at the back door. "Hi, honey," she said, hugging Corey. "I'm so happy you're back. Wait till you see what I've been working on in the barn."

Excitement rippled through Corey. For the past few months, her mother had been promising to build a bigger stall for Samurai. Mom finally got around to doing it! Corey thought.

Eagerly she followed her mother out to the barn. She couldn't wait to see Sam's new stall. Corey's pet goat, Alexander, loved spending time with Sam. He would enjoy the extra space, too.

But to Corey's surprise, Doc Tock didn't lead Corey to a new stall for Samurai. She led Corey to Samurai's *old* stall.

"Here we are, Corey." She opened the door with a proud expression.

"But . . ." Corey peered into the stall. Then she glanced back at her mother, puzzled. "Where's Sam?"

Doc Tock beamed at her. "Oh, I sold Samurai, honey. He's such a big pony, and we need the extra room for . . ."

Corey glanced into the stall again. "Bookshelves?" she said in disbelief.

"That's right, honey," her mother replied. "Isn't it wonderful?"

Corey couldn't believe it. Lining the walls of Sam's stall were rows and rows of shelves. On all the shelves were hundreds of copies of Alice's favorite book, *Harriet the Spy*!

"No! No!" Corey cried in horror. "No!"

Corey tossed and turned, tangling her legs in the sheets. At last her eyes flew open. She sat bolt upright in bed.

"Oh my gosh!" she gasped. She wasn't out in the barn looking at Samurai's empty stall. She was in bed, having a terrible, terrible nightmare.

"Thank goodness," she whispered.

Relieved, she lay down again. But her fingers were still trembling. Her heart was pumping hard. It was just a dream, but it had felt so real. . . .

It took a long time for Corey to relax again. When her eyes finally closed, it was almost midnight.

This time, as Corey drifted off to sleep, she didn't have a nightmare. She had a dream—a sweet dream—about a big moving van parked in front of the Lees' house.

"Where are the Lees going?" May asked in Corey's dream.

28

"Oh, far, far away," Corey answered. She smiled happily as the moving van drove past her house. "Isn't it wonderful, May?" Corey said to her friend. "Alice and her father are moving to Mars."

4 A Secret Friend

The next morning Corey was still lost in her dreams when an impatient voice woke her.

"Corey Takamura! This is the third time I've called you!"

Corey's eyes popped open. Her mother stood in the doorway of her bedroom. There was an annoyed expression on Doc Tock's face.

"If you don't get up right now, you're going to be late for school," Doc Tock said. "And I'm sure I don't have to remind you—there are some very hungry animals out in the barn waiting for their breakfast."

One of Corey's daily chores at her mother's house was to feed Samurai and Alexander. This week Corey was also responsible for feeding the litter of puppies. They were eight weeks old and had just started eating dog food.

Corey sprang out of bed. "Sorry, Mom," she said. "Don't worry. I'll get everything done."

As Doc Tock closed the door, Corey raced around her room, getting dressed and gathering her things to take to her father's that afternoon.

Downstairs, Corey gulped down a bowl of cereal. She had found all her books and a board game she wanted to take to her father's apartment, but her math homework was missing.

"Maybe I left it on the dining room table," she said to herself. That was where she'd done the homework two nights before.

As usual, there were all sorts of things piled up on the Takamuras' dining room table: yesterday's mail, a stack of Doc Tock's patients' charts, and a bunch of old magazines.

Corey dug through the mail. A few minutes later she fished her math papers out from under a pile of newspapers.

"Whew," she said, relieved. Her teacher wouldn't be very happy if Corey showed up at school without her math homework.

Corey scooped up the papers and shoved them into her notebook. Then she grabbed her backpack and gave her mother a quick kiss good-bye. She was still holding the notebook in her hands as she dashed out to the barn. If she hurried, she'd have just enough time to feed the animals before running to the bus stop.

"I'm coming, everybody," Corey called out as she approached the barn. "Your breakfast will be ready in a minute."

She was so worried about being late to feed the puppies and her pony and goat that she didn't see another of her pets racing in her direction. As she went into the barn, Dracula jumped up to say hello. His two huge front paws landed on Corey's chest, knocking her down. Her math notebook sailed out of her arms and landed on the ground with a thud. Papers flew everywhere.

"Oh no!" Corey cried. "My math homework!"

Dracula's tail stopped wagging. His eyes looked worried as he gave Corey one of his wet, slobbery kisses.

"It's not your fault, Dracula," she told him with a sigh. "I'm the one who wasn't watching where she was going."

She stood up and brushed off the seat of her jeans. She was about to chase after the math papers when a whinny came from the back of the barn. A loud, unhappy bleat followed. Samurai and Alexander were telling her that they were hungry—very hungry.

Corey glanced at the papers skittering across the yard. My math papers will have to wait, she decided. It wasn't fair to keep the hungry animals waiting one more minute for their breakfast.

She headed over to Samurai's stall. "Good morning, Alexander." The black-and-white goat trotted over, and she patted him on the head. "I'm sorry I'm so late." She turned to say hello to Samurai. After last night's nightmare, she couldn't help feeling relieved to see that Sam was still there, inside his stall.

Samurai blinked his big brown eyes at Corey, as if to say "What took you so long?"

Corey apologized to him, too. "I had a bad dream last night," she explained. "That's why I overslept this morning."

Corey moved quickly. She poured out fresh grain and water for Samurai. Then she dumped pellets into Alexander's bowl. After getting their breakfast ready, she hurried over to feed the litter of puppies. They yelped and scratched at their pen as Corey unlatched the gate. They were just as hungry as the goat and pony.

When Corey was finished feeding the puppies, she went back to Sam and Alexander to say good-bye. She wanted to let them know that May and Jasmine would be taking care of them while she was at her father's for the next few days.

On her way out of the barn, Corey

glanced at the clock on the stable wall. She was very late.

"I'm definitely going to miss the bus today," she mumbled. By the time she finished running around picking up her math papers, the bus would be long gone.

But when she reached the entrance of the stable, she gasped. "Oh my gosh . . ."

Her notebook was sitting right where she had dropped it. But it wasn't the disorganized mess that Corey had left behind. Instead, the cover of the spiral-bound notebook was closed, and all Corey's math papers were neatly tucked inside.

Corey glanced around. Her mother was busy with a patient, so she hadn't been the one to help Corey. Then who . . . ?

Dracula rubbed his nose against Corey's leg.

"It wasn't you, was it, Dracula?" Corey asked.

Just then she spotted her two best friends racing across Jasmine's backyard. They were headed for the bus stop, too.

"That's who," Corey said out loud. A big smile spread across her face. "Wait up!" she cried, running after her friends.

May and Jasmine turned around. They stopped when they saw Corey racing toward them.

"You two are the best," Corey declared.

"Of course we're the best!" May said, grinning.

"No, I mean it, May." Corey shook her head to show that she was serious. "I can't believe you did that for me."

Jasmine gave Corey a puzzled look. "Did what?"

"Picked up my papers, silly!" Corey said. "If you guys hadn't straightened up my notebook, I'd still be back at the barn, doing it myself."

"I don't know what you're talking about, Corey," said May. "We didn't pick up your papers."

Corey grinned. "It certainly wasn't Dracula!"

May and Jasmine exchanged looks.

"That's okay. You guys don't have to admit it," Corey went on. "I just want you to know that I really appreciate it."

As the girls joined the group of kids standing at the bus stop, Corey glanced across the street at the tall brick house with green shutters.

May saw Corey looking at Alice's house. "So how was it?" she asked.

"It was awful!" Corey told her friends about how rude Alice had been. When she got to the part about Alice saying that ponies were dumb and so was riding them, Jasmine gasped.

"I can't believe she said that!"

"She's the one who's dumb, Corey," May agreed. "I wouldn't want to spend time with her, either."

"I'm never going out to dinner with her again," Corey said solemnly. "As far as I'm concerned, Alice Lee is the most horrible, terrible—"

"Shhh!" Jasmine gripped Corey's arm. "Here she comes," she whispered.

Corey snapped her mouth closed. As she glanced across the street again, she

saw Alice and Kyle Lee walking down their driveway toward their car. For a second Alice's eyes met Corey's. Then the other girl looked away as she and her father climbed into their car.

"I hope Alice couldn't tell we were talking about her," Jasmine said in a worried tone.

"I don't think she could, Jasmine," May answered. "She was all the way across the street."

"But it was so obvious," Jasmine said. "We all stopped talking the second she walked out her front door."

Just then the Jeep backed out of the driveway. Kyle waved at the Pony Tails as he drove past their bus stop, but Alice was staring downward.

"She's probably got her nose in a book again," Corey said.

But Jasmine shook her head. "Didn't you see her face, Corey? Alice *must* have known we were talking about her."

"Why do you say that, Jasmine?" May asked.

"She was crying," Jasmine told them.

Corey felt her face flush. For a second she felt bad because she might have done something to make Alice cry. But her feeling quickly turned to anger as she remembered Alice's words last night. "I hope she did know we were talking about her," Corey said. She watched the Jeep continue down the street. "It serves her right for all the mean things she said to me."

Jasmine looked surprised by Corey's sharp tone. Before she could say anything more, the bus rounded the corner.

Corey bent down to pick up her backpack. By the time she stood up again, the black Jeep had disappeared.

5 The Secret Friend Strikes Again

Corey was at her father's apartment for the next few days. She was so busy with schoolwork and doing things with her father that she forgot about what had happened with Alice. In fact, she didn't think about Alice, or about Kyle, at all—until she returned to her mother's house.

"Kyle and I heard the most wonderful concert in Washington, D.C., this weekend," Doc Tock said at breakfast on Monday morning. "A marching band performed, and then we went to dinner at a seafood restaurant that Kyle and Alice like."

"A seafood restaurant?" Corey bit into a blueberry muffin. "Did Alice order *crab* for dinner?"

Doc Tock raised her eyebrows. "Alice was staying with her mom this weekend."

"Oh," Corey said. She stared at the back of a box of bran cereal. She wasn't really interested in hearing about Alice's weekend.

Luckily, Doc Tock changed the subject. "Thanks for feeding the puppies," she said. "You remembered to latch the gate on the pen—right?"

"Uh . . ." Corey hesitated. Last week while Corey was at her father's, Doc Tock's assistant, Jack, had been the one to feed the puppies. Twice he'd forgotten to latch the gate, and several of the puppies had found their way out into the Takamuras' yard. Corey knew her mother was worried that if the puppies escaped again, they might wander farther away.

Corey definitely remembered opening the pen to feed the puppies. And she definitely remembered shutting the gate. She just couldn't remember latching it.

She didn't want to admit that to her mother. "Of course I locked the gate, Mom," she said instead.

Doc Tock smiled at her. "I knew I could count on you, Corey," she said. "You're always such a big help around here."

Her mother's kind words immediately made Corey feel guilty about telling a lie. Doc Tock *did* count on Corey for help with her animal patients. Corey didn't want to let her down. And she didn't want anything to happen to the litter of cute puppies.

Corey left the last bit of muffin on the plate as she hurried out the back door again.

What if I didn't latch the gate? she worried. What if the puppies *did* run away? They're still so little, and so many terrible things could happen. By the time she reached the barn, Corey was sure she'd forgotten to latch the gate.

But as she approached the puppy

pen, she could make out several balls of yellow fur in the straw. Quickly she counted them. ". . . four . . . five . . . six . . . Thank goodness!" She let out a relieved breath as she realized that all eight Labs were there. She reached over to secure the gate.

Suddenly her fingers froze. The latch was already fastened!

Corey was positive that she'd left the gate unlocked. That meant only one thing.

"They did it again!" Corey exclaimed. "I am so lucky to have best friends like May and Jasmine—aren't I, little guy?" she said to one of the puppies. He waggled his tail in reply.

This wasn't the first time this morning that May and Jasmine had come to Corey's rescue. When she'd come out earlier to feed Sam and Alexander, both animals had already been munching contentedly on their breakfasts. And last week while Corey was at her father's, May and Jasmine had put her bike back in the garage for her. Yesterday the two

of them had even put Corey's tennis racket on her porch so that it wouldn't get soaked in the rain.

Corey wasn't sure why her best friends were helping her out so much lately, but she had a hunch. May and Jasmine were probably trying to help her forget about the situation with Alice.

Corey smiled as one of the puppies playfully bit another one. Together the two yellow Labs rolled around in the straw. The puppies are so cute, Corey thought. And thanks to May and Jasmine, they were also safe and sound.

"It's my turn to do something nice for May and Jasmine," Corey told the puppies.

As she headed back to the house to collect her things for school, a wonderful idea came to her. She knew just how to thank her secret helpers.

6 The Friendship Party

Corey waited until after school to put her plan into action.

"I'll meet you guys in May's barn in an hour, okay?" she said to May and Jasmine as the three of them got off the school bus together.

"Why do you want to meet in my barn?" May asked curiously. "Is this a special Pony Tails meeting or something?"

"Sort of." A mysterious grin spread across Corey's face. "Just meet me there in an hour," she said. "Then you'll find out what's going on!"

Before her friends could ask any

more questions, Corey turned around and raced into her house. As she burst into the kitchen, her mother looked up.

"Whoa!" Doc Tock said. "Where are you rushing to, Corey?"

"Hi, Mom!" Corey replied. "I have something really important to do. Can you help me make marshmallow treats?"

"Sure," Doc Tock said, reaching for the box of rice cereal. "I'm sure you'll tell me what this is about while we're cooking."

Corey filled her mother in as she began melting the margarine.

*   *   *

An hour later, Corey headed back across her backyard. In one hand she balanced a tray heaped with marshmallow treats and paper cups. In her other hand she held a pitcher of ice-cold juice.

As she entered the Grovers' barn, May and Jasmine were waiting for her in an empty box stall.

"All right!" May cheered when she

saw the goodies in Corey's arms. "A party!"

"A party?" Jasmine echoed. "But none of us is having a birthday, Corey."

"This is a best-friendship party," Corey explained proudly. "You guys have been doing so many nice things for me. It's my turn to do something nice for you." She sat down in the straw and began handing out cups. "Now, let's dig in!"

May sat down. "I'm not sure we really deserve this," she said. "But I'm certainly not going to refuse my favorite snack!"

As the girls munched on marshmallow treats and sipped juice, Corey tried to thank her friends again for their good deeds.

"Honestly, Corey," said Jasmine, "we didn't pick up your papers."

"And we didn't latch the puppy pen or feed Sam and Alexander for you," May said. "I'm not sure who your secret friend is, Corey, but it isn't us."

Corey shook her head. No matter how many times she told May and Jasmine how grateful she was for their help, they wouldn't listen. Instead, they kept repeating that they hadn't done all the nice things Corey knew they were doing.

A few minutes later, Corey decided to let the subject drop.

May helped herself to another marshmallow treat. "So is your mom still dating Kyle?" she asked.

Corey sighed. "She sure is. In fact, they're going to the movies this weekend with Alice." She made a face. "Luckily, Mom didn't ask me to come along!"

"I have a friend who goes to Fenton Hall," May said. "She told me that Alice sits all by herself at lunchtime. She doesn't talk to anybody; she just reads."

"I'm not surprised." Corey rolled her eyes. "If she were nicer, she'd have more friends."

May nodded. "She loves to read. Maybe she should read a book about how to stop being a total loser!"

Corey and Jasmine giggled.

Corey knew the Pony Tails weren't being very nice, but she didn't care. She had tried being nice to Alice once, and it hadn't worked.

"If I were a pony, I'd stomp on her foot, too!" Corey said. "Then I'd step on her other foot even harder!"

Laughter filled the barn.

"Why doesn't she get a haircut?" Jasmine said. "Her bangs are always in her eyes."

"I know," May agreed. "She looks as shaggy as Macaroni. And her clothes are so . . ." May's voice trailed off for a second. "Did you guys hear that?"

Corey had heard something, too, a muffled sound coming from above. She glanced up at the loft, where the Grovers stored supplies.

The sound came again. This time Corey thought it sounded like someone coughing.

"My sisters better not be eavesdropping on us again!" May said, getting to her feet. Corey and Jasmine followed as May began climbing the ladder that led to the loft.

As Corey reached the top rung behind May, she let out a loud gasp.

It wasn't May's sisters who were spying on the Pony Tails.

It was Alice Lee.

7 Alice the Spy

This time Corey wished she were having a bad nightmare. But this wasn't a nightmare—this was real.

Alice sat huddled in the straw behind several bales of hay. Her hands covered her face, but Corey could still see the tears streaming down her cheeks. A small notebook lay by her feet.

"You were spying on us!" May accused Alice.

Corey had a sick feeling in her stomach. Alice had been up in the loft, listening to the Pony Tails' conversation, the whole time. Alice had heard the Pony

Tails making fun of how she liked to read. She had heard them laughing at her long bangs. She had heard Corey say that if she were a pony she would stomp on Alice's foot.

As Alice dropped her hands, Corey could see that her eyes were red from crying. "You were talking about me!" Alice shot back at May.

Corey tried to say something, but her tongue felt as if it were made of lead.

"We're sorry, Alice," Jasmine said softly.

"No, we're not!" May said loudly. "This is my stable. You had no right to be here unless you were invited."

For a moment a terrible silence hung over the barn.

Then Alice leaped up. She flew past the three girls and scurried down the ladder. Corey watched through a window as Alice stumbled across May's yard.

"I can't believe her!" May said, fuming. "How dare she sneak into my barn and spy on us!"

"I wish we hadn't been talking about her," Corey murmured. She dropped down onto a bale of hay. She was angry, too. But she was also embarrassed. No matter how much Corey disliked Alice, she hadn't wanted Alice to overhear the mean things they had been saying about her.

Just then Corey noticed something lying in the straw. She bent over to pick it up.

Jasmine spotted it, too. "Is that Alice's notebook?" she asked.

Corey nodded. As she held the notebook in her hand, Corey couldn't help seeing something that was written on the open page. It was the word *Sam*. Before she could stop herself, her eyes scanned the rest of the words on the page.

Corey feeds Sam and Alexander every morning before she goes to school. Sam has grain and fresh water. Alexander eats pellets. I went into the stable to visit them again this morning. Sam is so handsome! His eyes are the color of hot fudge, and there's a white, curved mark on his nose. Today he and the puppies even seemed to recognize me. I'm getting more used to them, and they're getting more used to me. . . .

Corey hadn't meant to read the notebook, but Sam's name had jumped out at her. Now her mind was a jumble of thoughts.

So Alice had been sneaking into Corey's barn, too. But why? Corey wondered. Why had Alice been watching her feed Sam and Alexander?

Suddenly something came to her. "Oh my gosh," she whispered. "It's Alice."

"What's Alice?" Jasmine asked, looking at Corey.

"Now I believe you two," Corey told her friends. "You really aren't the ones who have been helping me. It's been Alice all along."

"You mean you think Alice is your secret friend?" May shook her head. "That doesn't make sense, Corey. Why would Alice do all those nice things for you?"

Corey hesitated. "I don't know," she admitted.

The Pony Tails were quiet for a moment.

"Maybe Alice doesn't really hate ponies," Jasmine said. "Maybe she's afraid of them. Helping you, Corey, was her way of apologizing—and trying to get used to being around animals."

Corey nodded thoughtfully. She had a feeling that Jasmine was right.

But when Corey climbed down the ladder a few minutes later, she felt more confused than before. Things were easier when I thought Alice was all bad, she realized.

Now that she knew Alice had a good side, Corey wasn't sure what to think—or do—about her.

8 Pony Club Day

The next morning, Corey put Alice's notebook in an envelope. Then she headed over to the Lees' house. She thought about putting a note in, too, but she still didn't know what to say to Alice.

Finally she decided to put only the envelope in the Lees' mailbox. She closed the lid, then hurried to join May and Jasmine at the bus stop. What will Alice think when she finds the notebook? Corey wondered. Will she realize that her secret has been found out?

* * *

Corey stayed with her father for the next few days. On Saturday Mr. Takamura drove her to Pine Hollow for the Horse Wise meeting.

"Is it supposed to rain *all* morning, Dad?" Corey moaned as they turned into the long driveway at Pine Hollow.

"I think so, honey," Mr. Takamura said. "It looks as if your trail ride will be postponed."

Corey stared glumly through the car window. She had been training Sam for the trail ride for the past two weeks. Now she would have to wait a while longer.

"Maybe Max has something fun planned for inside," Mr. Takamura said, trying to cheer her up. He stopped the car in front of the stable.

"I hope so," Corey said. She kissed her father good-bye, then raced across the muddy ground.

As Corey entered the stable, she inhaled the scent of fresh hay and horses. Immediately her spirits lifted. Even if it was raining outside, there was nothing better than being here at Pine Hollow, among so many horses and ponies.

Corey stood in the doorway of Max's office for a minute, glancing around at the people who were already in the room.

"Good morning, Corey," Max said. Max Regnery was the Pony Club leader, as well as the girls' riding instructor and the owner of Pine Hollow Stables. He grinned when he noticed Corey looking around. Then he pointed to a spot across the room.

Corey followed his finger. Sure enough, Max was pointing to where her two best friends were sitting cross-legged on the floor. "Thanks, Max," Corey said, smiling back at him.

"My pleasure," he replied.

"Sorry we couldn't bring Sam over today," May whispered as Corey sat down on the floor next to the other Pony Tails. Whenever they were going to ride at their Horse Wise meeting, May's father brought the ponies over in his horse trailer. "Once we saw the rain, we knew we wouldn't be riding today."

"I'm sorry, too," Corey told May. "But I'll see Sam later, at my mother's house." She smiled. "I'm still glad it's Pony Club day."

May nodded her agreement.

Just then Max clapped his hands. "Horse Wise, come to order!" he said.

Almost immediately the room grew quiet. Corey thought Max was a very good riding teacher. He was fun but strict, and expected a lot of his riders. Right now he expected them to be quiet while he spoke.

"As most of you could figure out," Max began, "we're not going to be able to take our trail ride today."

Several riders booed.

Max put a finger to his mouth to hush them. "We'll reschedule our trail ride," he promised. "In the meantime, I've got something fun planned."

"What is it?" Jackie Rogers asked eagerly.

"Spring cleaning day," Max told her.

"Spring cleaning day!" Stevie Lake echoed. She screwed up her face.

"That's not fun, Max!" Stevie was one of the most experienced riders at Pine Hollow. She and her friends, Lisa Atwood and Carole Hanson, were the members of The Saddle Club.

Everyone, including Max, laughed at Stevie's pained expression. His blue eyes twinkled. "I know cleaning is torture for some of us, Stevie," he said. "But there will be a reward afterward, I promise!"

For the next few minutes, Max told the riders about all the chores that needed to be done. The box stalls had to be mucked out; tack needed to be polished; the stable floor was dusty; and Max wanted the refrigerator scrubbed. "Inside and out," he added firmly. Corey listened as he listed about a dozen more jobs.

May raised her hand. "Can we work in groups?" she asked.

"Sure," Max told her.

The Pony Tails exchanged happy smiles. Spring cleaning day at Pine Hollow wasn't the most exciting event that

Horse Wise participated in, but the three friends were glad they could do it together.

"So what's our reward?" Stevie asked Max when he had finished telling the riders about the jobs.

"I hope it's chocolate!" said Jessica Adler.

"It's something even better," Max promised. "Well, almost better," he admitted. "It's Horse Charades."

"All right!" Jasmine cheered.

A few other riders brightened, too. The Pony Club had played Horse Charades several times before, and the game was lots of fun. One rider acted out something to do with horses while the other riders had to guess what it was.

"The sooner we finish cleaning, the sooner we can start playing," Max announced. "Let's get to it, everybody."

The riders scattered about the stable. Corey got to her feet and gazed around. Several older riders had already grabbed rakes and were mucking out stalls. Jessica Adler was sweeping the stable floor. Amie Connor and Jackie Rogers were dusting the riders' cubbies.

"Maybe we should clean out the refrigerator," Corey suggested to her friends. "That doesn't sound too hard, and we can do it together."

May and Jasmine agreed.

But by the time the Pony Tails reached the refrigerator, Carole Hanson and her friend Lisa Atwood were already scrubbing it out with sponges and buckets of soapy water.

Next the Pony Tails headed to the tack room. Max had mentioned several chores that needed to be done there. But Simon Atherton and Meg Durham were polishing the saddles. Veronica diAngelo and another rider had started to untangle a clump of knotted reins.

Corey was about to suggest another one of the chores on Max's list when May pointed to a shelf stacked with horse blankets.

"Why don't we fold the blankets?" she suggested.

"They're already folded, May," Jasmine pointed out.

"Yes, but not very neatly," May replied.

Corey hesitated. Folding blankets was definitely not one of the chores Max had mentioned. Besides that, the blankets didn't look very messy.

"Come on, you two," May urged her friends. "Most of the other chores are already taken. Besides, this is a good place for us to talk."

"Okay," Jasmine agreed.

Corey gave in, too. May was right. It *was* a quiet place to talk. Corey hadn't seen much of her friends in the past few days. She'd been hoping to talk over what to do about Alice.

Corey and Jasmine helped May pull down the blankets. Together the three of them unfolded the first one and folded it back up into a neat square. Then they carried it over to the shelf.

"There!" May said happily. "It looks much better."

Corey and Jasmine exchanged glances. At least one of them thought they had chosen a necessary chore.

As Corey and her friends unfolded

the next blanket, she brought up the topic of Alice.

"We haven't seen her since that day in May's barn," Jasmine told Corey. "Maybe she's been staying at her mother's house."

"I know you feel bad about what happened, Corey," May said. "But I still think Alice owes us an apology. If she hadn't sneaked into the barn, she never would have heard us talking about her."

"I guess so. . . ." Corey reached for another blanket, thinking about what May had said. Maybe May was right. Maybe the whole thing *was* Alice's fault. She'd definitely started the trouble that night at Sir Loyne's.

Just then Max came into the tack room. "How's the spring cleaning going?" he called out.

Simon Atherton pushed up his glasses and peered at Max. "Splendidly," he said.

Veronica diAngelo nodded. "Everything's fine."

"Great." Max glanced over at the Pony Tails. "How about you . . ." When he saw the chore they had chosen, he did a double take. "What are you three doing?"

"We're straightening up the blankets," May told him proudly. She pointed to the neat stack on the shelf. "Don't they look much neater, Max?"

"Well, yes, May," Max said. "They do look neater. But to tell you the truth, I can think of a million more important jobs that the three of you could be doing right now." He looked at Corey. "Jessica's out there sweeping all by herself. Why don't you go help her, Corey? Jasmine and May, finish what you're doing and then grab brooms, too."

"Okay, Max," Corey said, feeling sheepish. She'd had a feeling that Max wouldn't approve of the chore May had chosen for them.

"Thanks," Max told her, smiling. "Believe me, four of you can get the job done a lot more quickly than one of you. When we're finished, we can start Horse Charades."

Max disappeared to check on other

riders' progress, and Corey headed for the supply closet.

Jessica Adler looked thrilled when she saw Corey approaching with a broom in her hands. "Oh, good," she said. "Help has arrived!"

"Jasmine and May are coming, too," Corey told her. "Max said four of us could get the job done a lot more quickly than one of us."

"That's for sure," Jessica agreed. "It's taking me forever to sweep the stable by myself."

Corey got to work sweeping up piles of dust and loose straw. As she pushed the broom along the floor, she kept thinking about what Max had just said. He was right. Pine Hollow was a big stable. Four people could sweep it a lot more quickly than one person.

Corey bent down to brush the dirt she'd collected into a dustpan.

There's only one of Alice, and three of you.

Corey froze as the thought popped into her head. Alice had been all alone

the other day while the three Pony Tails were together having a party.

A party to thank May and Jasmine for things that Alice had done, Corey realized.

Corey stood up and dumped the dirt into the trash can.

When May and Jasmine came over a few minutes later to help with the sweeping, Corey pulled her two friends aside.

"Can you come to my house for a Pony Tails meeting this afternoon?" she asked.

"Sure." Jasmine nodded.

"What's up?" May asked.

"The Pony Tails have another job to do," Corey explained.

9 Corey Makes a Phone Call

"I think it's a great idea, Corey," Jasmine said enthusiastically. She turned to May. "What do you think?" she asked.

The three Pony Tails were at Corey's house after the Horse Wise meeting.

Corey watched May's face closely. She knew Jasmine was ready for the Pony Tails to call Alice, but she wasn't so sure about May. This morning May had insisted again that Alice was the one who'd done something wrong.

"You know what?" May said, looking at Corey. Corey shook her head. "I think you're right, Corey," May said finally. "After Alice helped you, we were really mean to her. Now it's our turn to do something nice for her."

A smile broke out on Corey's face. "Thanks, May." She gave her friend a quick hug. May could be stubborn sometimes, but she could also be very fair.

"Go ahead, Corey." Jasmine handed her the receiver. "Do it."

Corey drew in a deep breath as she took the phone, then dialed the Lees' phone number. What if Alice hangs up on me? Corey thought. What if she won't even talk to me?

"Hello?" Alice answered the phone.

Corey swallowed hard. "Hi, Alice," she blurted out. "It's Corey."

A long pause followed.

Butterflies fluttered inside Corey's stomach. "We're really sorry," she said in a rush. "May and Jasmine and I didn't mean to say all those nasty things about you. It's just . . . I guess I was really angry at you for what you said about ponies."

There was another long silence.

Nervously Corey pressed the phone

against her ear. All the terrible things the Pony Tails had said about Alice were replaying in her mind. Was Alice remembering them, too? If she was still angry and hurt, Corey couldn't blame her.

At last Alice cleared her throat. "It's okay, Corey," she said in a soft voice. "I know why you said those things about me." She paused. "I was pretty nasty to you, too. And I shouldn't have been hiding in May's loft in the first place."

Relief flooded over Corey. She flashed May and Jasmine a thumbs-up as Alice continued talking.

"Thanks for returning my notebook." Alice sounded a little embarrassed.

"I only read one page, honest, Alice," Corey said quickly. "That's how I figured out that you're my secret friend. If you hadn't picked up my math papers that day, I definitely would have missed the bus."

"I know." Alice laughed. "I was watching from inside your barn. I saw Dracula knock you down."

"He didn't mean to," Corey said. "He was just being friendly."

"I know that now, too," Alice said. "I don't really think ponies are dumb, Corey," she added hesitantly. "I . . . just don't know much about them. I'm not used to being around animals the way you and your mom are. That's the reason why I've been hanging around your barn so often. I've been trying to get used to them."

"Well . . ." Corey smiled at May and Jasmine as she began telling Alice the Pony Tails' idea. "I think we can help you with that."

"Help me?" Alice repeated. "How?"

"Can you meet us in May's barn at nine o'clock tomorrow morning?" Corey asked.

"Sure," Alice replied. "But . . ."

By the time Corey had finished explaining her idea, Alice sounded just as excited as Corey was.

10 The First Official Pony Ride

"What if Alice changes her mind and doesn't come?" Jasmine asked anxiously as the three Pony Tails met outside May's barn early the next morning.

"Don't be silly, Jasmine. Of course she'll come," May said. She reached up and carefully placed the saddle on Macaroni's back. "I bet she can't wait!"

Corey couldn't help smiling at May's answer. At first May hadn't wanted to apologize to Alice. But now that she had made up her mind that it was the right thing to do, she was just as eager to help Alice as Corey and Jasmine were.

Corey's palms were sweaty. She was excited, but nervous too. What if it doesn't work? she thought. What if Alice thinks this is a terrible idea?

Corey glanced at her watch. In another half hour, Corey would know how Alice was going to react.

At nine o'clock, the Pony Tails spotted someone hurrying across Corey's backyard.

"Here she comes!" Corey whispered.

"Ready, Macaroni?" May asked her pony.

He snorted his reply.

"He's ready!" Jasmine said confidently.

A moment later, Alice reached the Grovers' barn. "Hi, everyone," she said shyly.

The Pony Tails smiled at her. For a few minutes, the four girls just stood there. Nobody said a word.

The last time they'd all been at the Grovers' barn, Corey remembered, Alice had heard the Pony Tails talking about her. They had caught her spying on them. That had been a terrible day. Corey was hoping that today would be much better. She stared down at the ground, trying to think of something to say.

Just then she noticed that Alice had on a pair of riding boots. "I like your boots," she said.

"Thanks," Alice replied. A little smile crept across her face. "I bought them when I signed up for riding lessons. But I never got to wear them again."

"Why not?" asked Jasmine.

"After that pony stepped on my foot, I stopped taking lessons." Alice glanced at Corey. "I hope you're not going to stomp on my foot."

Corey blushed as she remembered what she'd said the other day. Then Alice started laughing. So did Corey.

"Corey won't step on your foot," May promised. "And neither will Macaroni. He's very gentle."

For the first time Alice's eyes drifted over to Macaroni. May's shaggy yellow pony was tied to the fence around the training ring. He blinked at Alice as she glanced his way.

"Macaroni won't throw me off his back—will he?" Alice asked.

"Macaroni is the nicest pony in the world," Jasmine reassured her.

"He's the best," Corey said. "Come on, Alice. We'll introduce you."

Slowly Alice followed the Pony Tails over to Macaroni.

"Here." May stuck a small bit of apple in Alice's hand. "If you give him this, he'll be your friend for life."

Corey saw Alice take a deep breath. Then she stepped toward the pony.

"Hello, Macaroni," Alice said softly. She looked into his gentle brown eyes. The pony shook his head a little, as if he were saying hello back to her. Cautiously Alice held out the bit of apple. Macaroni reached over and took it. Then he nuzzled Alice's palm, looking for more.

"He likes it!" Alice exclaimed.

"He *loves* it," May corrected her. "Here. Give him another one."

When Macaroni was finished with his treat, Alice petted his soft head. "He's so shaggy," she commented. "And his coat is just the color of—"

"Macaroni and cheese," the three Pony Tails said at once.

Alice laughed. "That's exactly what I was going to say!"

"Give us a high five, a low five, and then shout 'Jake,'" May told her. "That's what we always do when we say the same thing at the same time."

The four girls did high fives, low fives, and then shouted "Jake" all at once.

Alice glanced at Corey. "I think I'm ready," she said.

Corey nodded. She and Jasmine helped Alice climb up into the saddle while May ran into the house to get her father. Mr. Grover was going to be the one to give Alice her first official pony ride.

"Good morning, Alice," Mr. Grover said as he came out the back door. "You're in for a real treat today." He reached for the lead line that the Pony

Tails had clipped to Macaroni. Slowly he led Macaroni and his rider into the ring.

The Pony Tails stood outside the ring, watching Alice and Macaroni.

Corey held her breath. Alice looked very nervous as she and Macaroni began to circle the ring. But after a few trips around, Corey could tell that Alice had relaxed into the saddle. Corey relaxed, too. Alice was doing exactly what Mr. Grover had told her to do, which was to let him and Macaroni do all the hard work.

"She's doing really well," Jasmine commented. "Good job, Corey."

"Thanks," Corey said happily. She thought Alice was doing well, too. In fact, she thought Alice was doing great.

May rested her chin on top of the fence as she watched her pony and Alice circling the ring. "Isn't Macaroni a wonderful pony?" she sighed.

"He sure is," Corey agreed. Macaroni was doing his job perfectly. He was not only showing his new rider that ponies were smart and sweet; he was showing her that they were fun to ride.

No wonder there's such a big smile on Alice's face, Corey thought.

Alice was loving every minute of her first official pony ride.

11 Training Parents

After a while, Alice's first official pony ride was over.

Mr. Grover helped Alice climb off Macaroni's back.

When Alice came over to talk to the Pony Tails, her cheeks were flushed and her brown eyes sparkled. "That was so much fun!" She smiled at Corey. "Thank you."

"You're welcome," Corey replied. She smiled back at her new friend.

"You can ride Macaroni anytime you want," May told Alice.

An odd look crossed Alice's face.

Then she shook her head. "Thanks, but I don't think so, May."

"But . . ." Corey felt her mouth drop open. Alice didn't want to ride Macaroni again? Corey had been so sure that Alice loved the pony ride.

"How can I ride Macaroni anytime I want?" Alice said, teasing May. *"You're always riding him!"*

May and Jasmine burst out laughing. As Corey joined in, she felt her whole body relax. Alice hadn't been saying she didn't want to ride Macaroni again. Alice had been cracking a joke!

Alice isn't unfriendly, Corey realized. She's just shy. Once you get to know her, she's even funny!

After that Alice helped the Pony Tails untack Macaroni, and together the four girls led him back into the stable. As they opened the pony's stall door, Corey couldn't help thinking of Max's reaction when he'd seen the three of them folding the blankets. If he saw them now, he would say that a simple job like untacking a pony and putting him away didn't require four riders, either.

But this time it feels right for four riders to do it together, Corey thought, smiling. She had a feeling that even Max would agree.

When Macaroni was back in his stall, it was time for Alice and Corey to go home for lunch. Together they crossed May's backyard and headed for Corey's house.

As they walked, Corey told Alice a little more about her work training Samurai.

"It sounds fun," Alice said.

"It is," Corey explained. "But it's hard work, too. And you have to be patient. If Samurai doesn't perform well the next time Horse Wise goes out on the trail, I'm going to have to keep practicing that exercise over and over."

Alice nodded thoughtfully. "It's too bad you can't train parents the way you can train ponies," she said suddenly.

Corey giggled. "Do you want to put

your dad in May's training ring?" she asked.

"Not exactly," Alice said, giggling too. "I was just thinking about how you're trying to teach Sam to follow your directions. I wish I could train my parents to follow my directions. That way they might get back together."

"Oh." Corey thought she was beginning to understand what Alice had meant.

"I really like your mother, Corey," Alice went on. "It's just . . . I can't get used to my dad going out on dates with her."

Now Corey was sure she understood. Alice was saying exactly what Corey had been feeling ever since her mother had started dating Kyle. "I know exactly what you mean," she said. "My parents have only been divorced for a little while. I'm still getting used to that. Now I have to get used to my mother's having a boyfriend!"

Alice shook her head. "Wasn't that dinner awful?" she asked, giggling a little again. "I promise I won't act like that the next time our parents make us come along on one of their dates."

Corey was about to agree. Then suddenly something occurred to her. "Hey! Maybe we *can* train our parents!" she exclaimed.

It was Alice's turn to be confused. "What do you mean, Corey?"

"Well, we can't exactly train our parents to follow our directions," Corey explained. "That only works with ponies. But maybe there's something else we can do."

Alice cocked her head. "I'm listening."

Corey's eyes twinkled. "What if you and I stay *secret* friends?" she said. "That way—"

"Our parents won't find out that we like each other and start dating each other even more!" Alice finished. She laughed out loud. "That's a brilliant idea, Corey."

Corey stuck out her hand. "I won't tell my mother that I like you, if you don't tell your father that you like me."

"It's a deal," Alice said. "As far as he's concerned, I can't stand you."

"Perfect," Corey announced.

Then the two secret friends shook on it.

COREY'S TIPS ON KEEPING A PONY JOURNAL

One of the nicest things about having a secret friend was having somebody who helped me take care of Samurai. In case you don't know it, taking care of a pony is a big job. There are some things I've learned to do that seem like a lot of work, but they really just save a lot *more* work—and trouble. One of them is keeping a journal. In a way, it's like Sam's diary, only I'm the one who has to put all the information in it because I can't read Sam's handwriting!

JANUARY	FEBRUARY	MARCH
15--Farrier at 10:30 21--Worming	21--Farrier at 1:00	15--Farrier at 10:30 28--Sam's Teeth
APRIL	MAY	JUNE
21--Farrier at 11:00	15--Farrier at 10:30 21--Shots!	7--Horse Show 21--Farrier at 1:00

The most important reason for keeping a journal is Sam's health care. Since the whole idea of health care is to keep him from getting sick, I have to be sure he's getting all his preventive care on schedule. Some things get done regularly, like shoeing, de-worming, and vaccinations. Every January, when I begin a new journal, I make a chart in the front to remind myself about all those. Then, when each of them gets done, I put a checkmark next to it. Then I also put all the information in the main part of the journal so I know exactly what's been done.

Sam's hooves grow like crazy, so the farrier—that's the name for a black-smith who takes care of horseshoes—has to come to look at his shoes and check his feet every six weeks. Some ponies only need to see the farrier every other month, but Sam's feet get uncomfortable if he doesn't get his hooves trimmed more often. I don't want Sam to be uncomfortable, ever.

Ponies are likely to get all kinds of parasites—that means bugs and worms that live in or on them. We have to give Sam regular treatments to keep him free of parasites. It's disgusting to think about, but it's even more disgusting to think about what would happen to him if we didn't do it. Mom and I can usually give Sam the medicine he needs for de-worming without the veterinarian's help, but I have to know when he's supposed to get it. So that goes in the journal, too.

Then, every year, Sam needs lots and lots of shots to keep him from getting sick. Judy Barker, the veterinarian, gives those to him, and she does it so well that he hardly even notices. Some of the most important ones protect him from tetanus and rabies. He gets those shots every year. I get a shot for tetanus, too—not from Judy, though. My pediatrician gives it to me. Mom says every kid should get regular tetanus shots, but it's especially important for kids who ride horses. My pediatrician gives me a lollipop when I get a shot, as long as I don't cry. I give Sam an apple when he gets a shot—as long as he doesn't cry!

Sam gets other shots, too, to protect him from sleeping sickness, flu, and other diseases horses can get. Judy helps us decide which shots he'll need and when he should get them. I put those dates on the chart, too.

All that information goes onto the chart when I make it up every January. The rest of the year, I fill in the pages of the journal. For Mom and Judy Barker and for Sam, I write down every time Judy comes to see Sam and every time he has any kind of health problem. That includes things like a sore ankle, but it also means making a note when Sam gets into a strange mood. Ponies are like people. They can get into moods, and a lot of the time, it doesn't mean anything at all. We all know that's especially true of Sam! Sometimes it does mean something, though, and that's another reason a journal can be really, really important. For instance, last year I noticed that I'd kept writing "cranky" in the journal right before the farrier came to trim Sam's hooves. That was how we realized that he needed to have the farrier come more often. He was cranky because his feet hurt! I might never have noticed that if I hadn't put something in the journal and then realized that there was a pattern.

I try to make a note of what I'm feeding Sam and how much he eats. I change his diet in different seasons, and it's important to have a record of when I make a change and what it is. I also make a note if he drinks a lot (he does, especially in hot weather) or sweats a lot (ditto). I even note when he seems particularly cheerful and cooperative.

I keep the journal on a shelf next to Sam's stall. There's a pencil and a pen there, too, attached by a string so I won't have to go hunting for something to write with every time I need to put something in the journal. Keeping the journal handy reminds me that I need to write in it.

Most of what I write in the journal is for Sam—his health, his diet, and so on. Some of it, though, is for me. I write down the things I'm working on and the things I'm learning. I know the first time I ever jumped with Sam, and I know the first time he bucked and threw me. I write down when the Pony Tails go on a picnic and when Sam's stablemate, Alexander, does something really cute. I write down when Sam is wonderful (that's just about every day) and when I miss him (when I'm at my dad's). One of the nice things about a journal is that I don't have to write much to remember a lot. The other day, Sam was very playful. There was a loose piece of yarn hanging from the sleeve of my red sweater, and every time I moved my arm, he watched it. His ears perked forward and his eyes opened wide. Then, when I walked away from him, he sort of chased after it and tried to nip at it. He was behaving just like a kitten with a ball of yarn. It was so cute! In the journal, I just wrote, "kitten." That one little word written there will always remind me of a very special time I had with my pony.

About the Author

Bonnie Bryant was born and raised in New York City, and she still lives there today. She spends her summers in a house on a lake in Massachusetts.

Ms. Bryant began writing about girls and horses when she started The Saddle Club series in 1987. So far there are more than sixty books in that series. Much as she likes telling the stories about Stevie, Carole, and Lisa, she decided that the younger riders at Pine Hollow Stables, especially May Grover, have stories of their own. That's how Pony Tails was born.

Ms. Bryant rides horses when she has time away from her computer, but she doesn't have a horse of her own. She likes to ride different horses, enjoying a variety of riding experiences. She thinks most of her readers are much better riders than she is!

*Don't miss Bonnie Bryant's next Pony
Tails adventure . . .*

JASMINE'S FIRST HORSE SHOW
Pony Tails #13

Jasmine is thrilled to be getting ready
for her first horse show. Then bad
things start happening. Her pony, Outlaw, can't be ridden. Her baby sister,
Sophie, gets sick and her parents have
to stay home to take care of her. Jasmine's first horse show is ruined before
it's even begun. Then Jasmine learns
that sometimes you can't get everything
you want, but life has a way of working
out anyhow.

Due in bookstores in August 1997!

Win riding lessons and a saddle!

Sweepstakes sponsored by

STATE LINE TACK®
The Discount Tack Store

Hurry— enter to win!

✂ -

Return completed entry to:
Bantam Doubleday Dell, Attn: Free Riding Lessons, 1540 Broadway, 20th floor, New York, NY 10036

Name _____

Address _____

City _____ State _____ Zip _____

Date of Birth _____ / _____ / _____
                               Month   Day   Year

HORSE CRAZY SWEEPSTAKES OFFICIAL RULES

I. ELIGIBILITY

No purchase necessary. Enter by completing and returning the Official Entry Form. All entries must be received by Bantam Doubleday Dell postmarked no later than July 15, 1997. No mechanically reproduced entries allowed. By entering the sweepstakes, each entrant agrees to be bound by these rules and the decision of the judges which shall be final and binding. Limit one entry per person.

The sweepstakes is open to children between the ages of 4 and 15 years of age (as of July 15, 1997), who are residents of the United States and Canada, excluding the Province of Quebec. The winner, if Canadian, will be required to answer correctly a time-limited arithmetic skill question in order to receive the prize. Employees of Bantam Doubleday Dell Publishing Group, Inc., and its subsidiaries and affiliates and their immediate family members are not eligible. Void where prohibited or restricted by law. Grand Prize will be awarded in the name of a parent or legal guardian.

II. PRIZE

The prize is as follows:

One Grand Prize: Approximate Retail Value - $1,000 consists of: $500 worth of riding lessons at the stable of your choice and one of the following three saddles: Collegiate Prep All-Purpose-Child's (retail: $435), Collegiate Alumnus All-Purpose-Adult (retail: $475), SLT Cambridge Prix D'Ecole-Adult (retail: $649).

III. WINNER

Winner will be chosen in a random drawing on or about August 15, 1997, from among all completed entry forms. Winner will be notified by mail. Odds of winning depend on the number of entries received. No substitution or transfer of the prize is allowed. All entries become the property of BDD and will not be returned. Taxes, if any, are the sole responsibility of the winner. BDD RESERVES THE RIGHT TO SUBSTITUTE A PRIZE OF EQUAL VALUE IF PRIZE, AS STATED ABOVE, BECOMES UNAVAILABLE. Winner and their legal guardian will be required to execute and return, within 14 days of notification, affidavit of eligibility and release. A non-compliance within that time period or the return of any prize notification as undeliverable will result in disqualification and the selection of an alternate winner. In the event of any other non-compliance with rules and conditions, prize may be awarded to an alternate winner. For a list of winners (available after August 15, 1997), send a self-addressed, stamped envelope entirely separate from your entry to: Bantam Doubleday Dell, Attn: Riding Winners, 1540 Broadway, 20th floor, New York, NY, 10036. Return completed entry to: Bantam Doubleday Dell, Attn: Free Riding Lessons, 1540 Broadway, 20th floor, New York, NY 10036.

BFYR 137